This igloo book belongs to:

. . . .

Contents

igloobooks

Published in 2016
by Igloo Books Ltd
Cottage Farm
Sywell
NN6 0BJ
www.igloobooks.com

LEO002 0416
4 6 8 10 9 7 5
ISBN: 978-1-78197-322-6

Printed and manufactured in China
Written by Melanie Hibbert

My Favourite
Bedtime
Stories

igloobooks

Bedtime for Bunnies

Dippy, Nippy and Pippy never liked getting ready for bed. "Come on, bunnies!" called their mother from the house. "It's bath time." The bunnies didn't want to go inside for a bath. They wanted to stay outside and play!

Dippy hopped behind the watering can. Nippy bounced behind the apple tree and Pippy dived into the washing basket. The bunnies tried to stay quiet, but they couldn't help giggling. "Come inside, bunnies, or there'll be no bedtime story," said Mum.

The bunnies didn't want to miss their bedtime story, so one by one, Dippy, Nippy and Pippy hopped upstairs to the bathroom. Pippy had a bath first. Then, Dippy and Nippy hopped in. They splished and splashed and had a lovely time.

6

After the bath, it was time for the bunnies to brush their teeth.
Pippy said she was hungry and wanted to nibble some lettuce.
Dippy moaned, "I'm thirsty, I want some carrot juice."
Then, Nippy squidged the toothpaste all over the floor!

It wasn't easy, trying to get three bouncy bunnies to bed.
"I've lost my daisy slippers," said Pippy, unhappily.
"It's cold," moaned Nippy, "I need a hot-water bottle."
"Can I please have a hug, Mummy?" asked Dippy.

Mum found Pippy's slippers, filled Dippy's hot-water bottle and gave Nippy a hug. "Now, off to bed," she said. "Dad is waiting to read you a bedtime story."
The bunnies loved Dad's stories, so they hopped upstairs and snuggled in bed.

9

Dad told Pippy, Dippy and Nippy about his adventures making dens and digging holes as a young bunny. "At bedtime, instead of going to bed," he said, "I would hop off to the farmer's field and nibble his prize carrots. Then, one evening, he caught me and chased me back to the burrow."

"What happened after that?" asked the curious bunnies.
"I always went to bed when I was told," replied Dad.
Then, he tucked the bunnies in tight, gave them a kiss and turned
off the light. "Goodnight, little bunnies. Sleep tight," he said.

Where's Panda?

Alex loved his toy, Panda, more than anything else in the world. Panda was black and white and soft and cute. Wherever Alex went, Panda went, too. If there was one thing that Alex couldn't imagine, it was being without his soft, black and white bear.

One day at the toyshop, Alex put Panda down and forgot where he'd left him. "Don't worry," said Mum. "We'll find him."
They searched all over the shop and found Panda sitting with the other cuddly toys. "Panda's found some friends," said Alex.

13

Another day, Panda got really muddy when he fell into a puddle.
"Panda needs a wash," said Mum, as she put him in the
washing machine. It went splish-splash, splish-splash. Alex didn't
like Panda being turned round and round.
"He might get dizzy!" he cried.

After that, when Alex had a bath, Panda had to have one, too.
"We'll be pirates, sailing the seven seas!" cried Alex.
He giggled and sploshed and covered Panda in bubbles.
"Now you're a sea monster!" he cried.

One evening, Alex looked everywhere, but Panda was nowhere to be found. So, Alex began to cry. He cried and cried and it got louder and louder. "I'VE LOST MY PANDA!"
"There, there," said Mum, giving Alex a cuddle.

Alex hopped into bed. He felt lost without Panda. Then, he felt something soft under his pillow. "I found Panda!" he cried. Mum smiled and gave Alex a kiss. "I love you, Mum. I love you, Panda," said Alex, snuggling down happily.

17

Sam's First Sleepover

Sam was going on his first ever sleepover. He was excited, but a little worried, too. "I'll be sleeping in a strange bed," he said to his mum. "What if I don't like it?"

"Don't worry," replied Mum, "you can take Yellow Bear to snuggle up with. He's soft and cuddly."

"Can I take my spacesuit pyjamas as well, Mum?" asked Sam.
"Of course," replied Mum. Then, she neatly packed Sam's
pyjamas, toothbrush and clean clothes for the morning.
Last of all, she remembered to tuck in Yellow Bear.

As soon as Sam arrived at his friend Tim's house, they rushed into the garden. They climbed up trees, whizzed down the slide, swung on an old tyre and built a secret den in the bushes. It was great fun and Sam felt really happy.

After playing all afternoon, Sam was feeling hungry.
Suddenly, Tim's mum shouted, "Come in, boys. It's dinner time!"
Tim's mum had made beans, chips and a delicious pie with
blueberry ice cream for pudding.

21

After dinner, Tim and Sam played hide-and-seek for ages.
"Boo, found you!" cried Tim, giggling. Sam crawled out from
under the table and gave a big yawn.
"Come on," said Tim's mum. "It's time for bed."

After brushing their teeth and putting on their pyjamas, the boys climbed into bunk beds. Sam was on the bottom one and couldn't see Tim above him. "Goodnight, boys," Tim's mum said, as she switched off the light.

Sam pulled the covers up. "Goodnight, Tim," he said. "Goodnight," replied Tim, sleepily. Soon, Tim was snoring gently. Sam looked around in the dark. Everything felt strange and he began to feel scared.

Sam missed his mum, until he remembered what she had said.
He crept out of bed and unpacked Yellow Bear. He snuggled up
with his soft, special friend who smelled of home. Before long,
Sam drifted into a deep sleep and dreamed happily about his
next sleepover.

Elsa's Magical Box

Elsa's tooth had been wobbling for ages. Then, one night before bed, it fell out. "Mum, my tooth fell out!" cried Elsa. Mum gave Elsa a small, silver box for her to put her tooth into.

Mum told Elsa to put the magic tooth box under her pillow. "The fairies will take the tooth away and leave a surprise in the morning," she said. So, Elsa hid the tooth box under her pillow and snuggled down.

"I wish I could see the fairies when they come," she said.
Elsa closed her eyes and felt herself drifting off to sleep.
Then suddenly, she heard little giggles and the fluttering of wings.
She opened her eyes to see little fairies flying all around.

28

"Come with us to Fairyland!" said the fairies. Magic sparkles twinkled and shone. Suddenly, Elsa was in an enchanted land. There were lemonade streams and candy trees and little fairies everywhere. They invited Elsa to a delicious fairy feast and afterwards everyone played lots of wonderful games.

29

The fairies gave Elsa her own wand. She changed mushrooms into flowers and leaves into little gold coins. "This is brilliant!" cried Elsa, as her wand went PING! She had fun playing for hours. Then, suddenly, Fairyland began to fade.

"It's time to go," said the fairies. "Goodbye, Elsa."

There was a burst of sparkles and POOF! Elsa woke up with a start to find herself back in her room. It was morning time, so Elsa opened the silver box. There, instead of her tooth, was a gold coin! "The box really is magic!" cried Elsa. From then on, whenever she lost a tooth, Elsa knew exactly what to do.

Bella's Babysitter

Bella's mum and dad were going out for the evening. "A babysitter will come and look after you until we get back," said Mum, "so don't worry." Bella had never had a babysitter before. She felt a bit worried, but she was quite excited, too.

Bella was wondering what the babysitter might be like, when, ding-dong, the doorbell rang. She hid behind a plant and peeped out, clutching her toy kitten. "Hello," said the babysitter, as Mum opened the door. Her voice sounded really nice.

Bella came out from her hiding place. "There you are," said Mum.
"Come and meet Tina. You'll have lots of fun together."
"Hello," said Tina, kindly. "I'm your babysitter."
"Hello," replied Bella, shyly. Ding-dong! The doorbell rang again.
It was Mum and Dad's taxi.

Bella didn't like it when her parents left. She felt a bit sad, but then Tina had a great idea. "Let's make some popcorn," she said. In the kitchen, Tina poured popping corn into a special cooker. Pop-pop-pop! Bella watched as puffs of popcorn bounced under the lid. "It's so much fun!" she squealed.

Tina made mugs of creamy hot chocolate and then, took the popcorn into the lounge where 'Sing-along with Tiger' was on TV. "I love this," said Bella. Tina and Bella danced and followed Tiger's actions. They burst out laughing and ate handfuls of delicious, buttery popcorn.

Soon, it was time to go to bed, but Bella didn't mind at all. Tina read her a bedtime story and then Bella snuggled down. "Goodnight, Tina," said Bella, sleepily. "You're a brilliant babysitter and I can't wait for you to come back."

Camping Out

Mum and Dad had bought Millie and Milo a lovely, red tent for their birthday. "Can we camp outside in it?" they asked.
"Yes," said Dad, "but I bet you'll be back in when it gets dark."

"We like the dark!" cried Millie, grabbing their sleeping bags.
Dad took the tent into the garden.
Milo scooped up cushions, games and torches.
The twins ran outside and dived into the tent, giggling.

Millie and Milo played games and pretended they were explorers in the jungle. When it got dark, Milo told the story of the moonlight monster. "He's furry and hairy and comes out at night," he whispered. Suddenly, outside, there was a noise.

A strange shadow moved along the tent. It got bigger and bigger. The tent flap moved. "It's the moonlight monster!" cried Millie. "No, it isn't," said Milo, giggling. "It's just Stripes the cat!"

41

"I'm not sure I like the dark," said Millie. Just then,
there was a funny rumbling sound. "What was that?"
asked Milo.
"It was my tummy rumbling!" said Millie.
"I'm a bit cold and I'm very hungry," she said.

42

So, Millie and Milo went inside where Mum and Dad were waiting. They all huddled together and had hot, buttered toast and cups of steaming hot chocolate. Milo and Millie liked camping out, but there was nothing better than snuggling up to Mum and Dad and listening to their stories.

Harvey the Explorer

Harvey was going to be a famous explorer. "I'll start in the garden," he said and went off, wearing his special explorer's kit. Harvey was creeping through the undergrowth when something fluttered around his head and landed on his nose.

"It's a butterfly," whispered Harvey, already holding his net.
The butterfly fluttered this way and that, round and round.
Harvey tried to catch it, but the butterfly flew away.
"I feel dizzy," he said and he sat on the grass.

Suddenly, there was a croak! Something green, with long legs, leaped out of the bushes.

"It's trying to get me!" shouted Harvey, but it was only a frog. He watched the frog as it hopped to the pond. "Croak, croak!"

Just then, Harvey felt a tickly feeling. It went from his toes,
up his leg, to his knees. It made him shiver and giggle.
Harvey looked through the magnifying glass.
"It's a monster!" he cried, but it was only a spider.

Suddenly, Mum called out from the kitchen. "It's hard work being an explorer, Harvey, would you like some orange juice and freshly baked cookies?"

Harvey couldn't get inside quickly enough. "Yes please," he said. "I've had enough of being an explorer. It's a jungle out there!"